SNEEZES

A-CHOO

Marilyn Singer

pictures by Brian Floca

HarperFestival®
A Division of HarperCollins Publishers

Solomon Snorkel has such a big sneeze,
he can blow all the leaves off
the sycamore trees.

He can empty the beehives of all of the bees.
That's what Solomon's sneezes can do.

**Solomon Snorkel has such a large sneeze,
he can knock several skiers
right out of their skis.**

He can break open locks,
so he doesn't need keys.
That's what Solomon's sneezes can do.

Solomon Snorkel has such a great sneeze,
he can topple a giant down onto his knees.

He can shear an old sheepdog
and scatter its fleas.
That's what Solomon's sneezes can do.

Solomon Snorkel has such
a strong sneeze,
from East Coast to West,
folks feel chilled by the breeze.

**And way up on Mars
they're afraid they might freeze.
That's what Solomon's sneezes can do.**

Solomon Snorkel has such a huge sneeze,
on top of the mountains and under the seas,
everyone quakes when they hear Solly wheeze
for they know what his sneezes can do.